This **Aussie Kids** book belongs to

....

who lives in

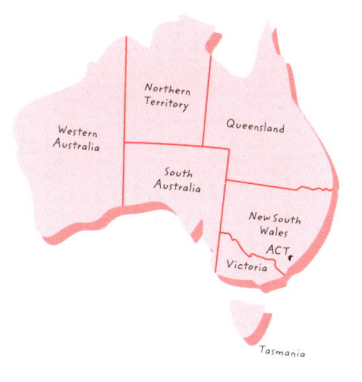

Northern Territory
Queensland
Western Australia
South Australia
New South Wales
ACT
Victoria
Tasmania

....

For Ian, who liked the kangaroo pages. *R.C.*
To Emma, James, Millie, Obie and Caspar, who love to explore this great part of Australia. Thank you for sharing your stories with me. *K.B.*

PUFFIN BOOKS

UK | USA | Canada | Ireland | Australia
India | New Zealand | South Africa | China

Penguin
Random House
Australia

Penguin Random House Australia is part of the Penguin Random House group of companies whose addresses can be found at global.penguinrandomhouse.com.

First published by Puffin Books, an imprint of
Penguin Random House Australia Pty Ltd, in 2020
Text copyright © Raewyn Caisley 2020
Illustrations copyright © Karen Blair 2020

The moral right of the author and illustrator has been asserted.

All rights reserved. No part of this publication may be reproduced, published, performed in public or communicated to the public in any form or by any means without prior written permission from Penguin Random House Australia Pty Ltd or its authorised licensees.

Cover and internal illustrations by Karen Blair
Design © Penguin Random House Australia Pty Ltd
Author photograph © Joanna Everitt, ImaJE Photography
Typeset in 18pt New Century Schoolbook by Midland Typesetters, Australia

Printed and bound in China

A catalogue record for this book is available from the National Library of Australia

ISBN 978 1 76089 410 8

Penguin Random House Australia uses papers that are natural and recyclable products, made from wood grown in sustainable forests. The logging and manufacture processes are expected to conform to the environmental regulations of the country of origin.

penguin.com.au

Aussie Kids

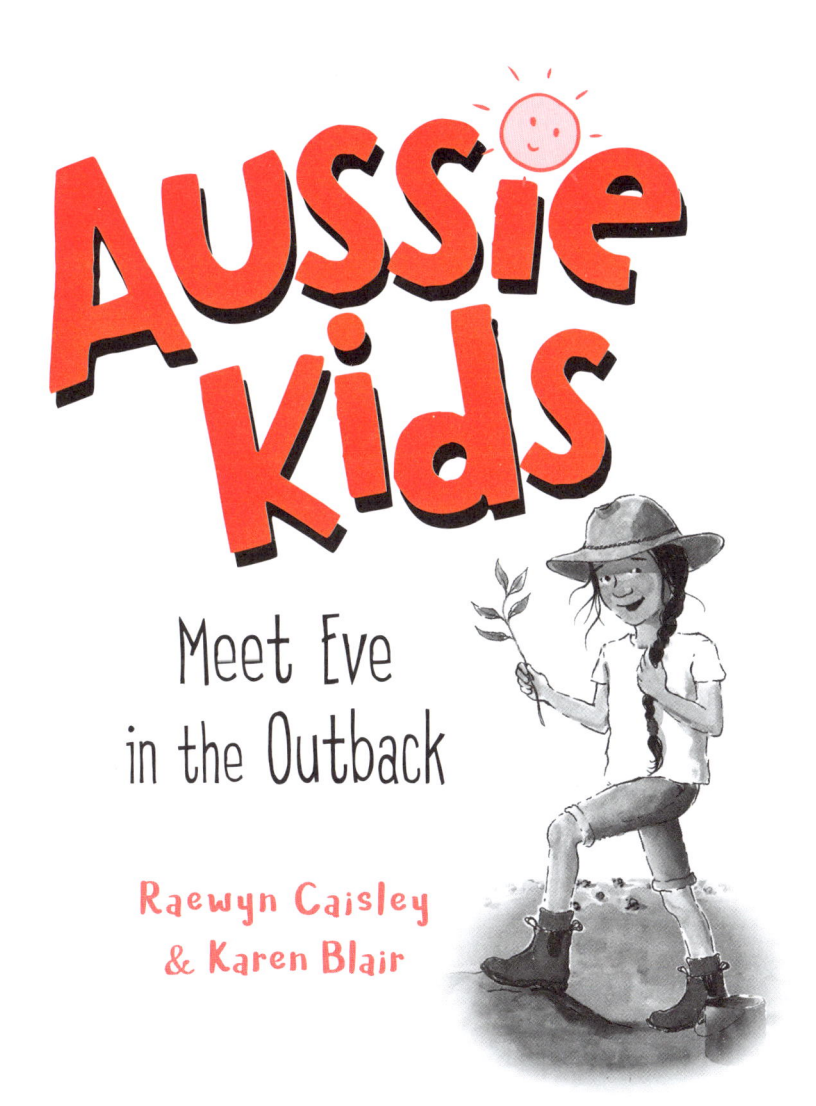

Meet Eve in the Outback

Raewyn Caisley & Karen Blair

PUFFIN BOOKS

Northern Territory

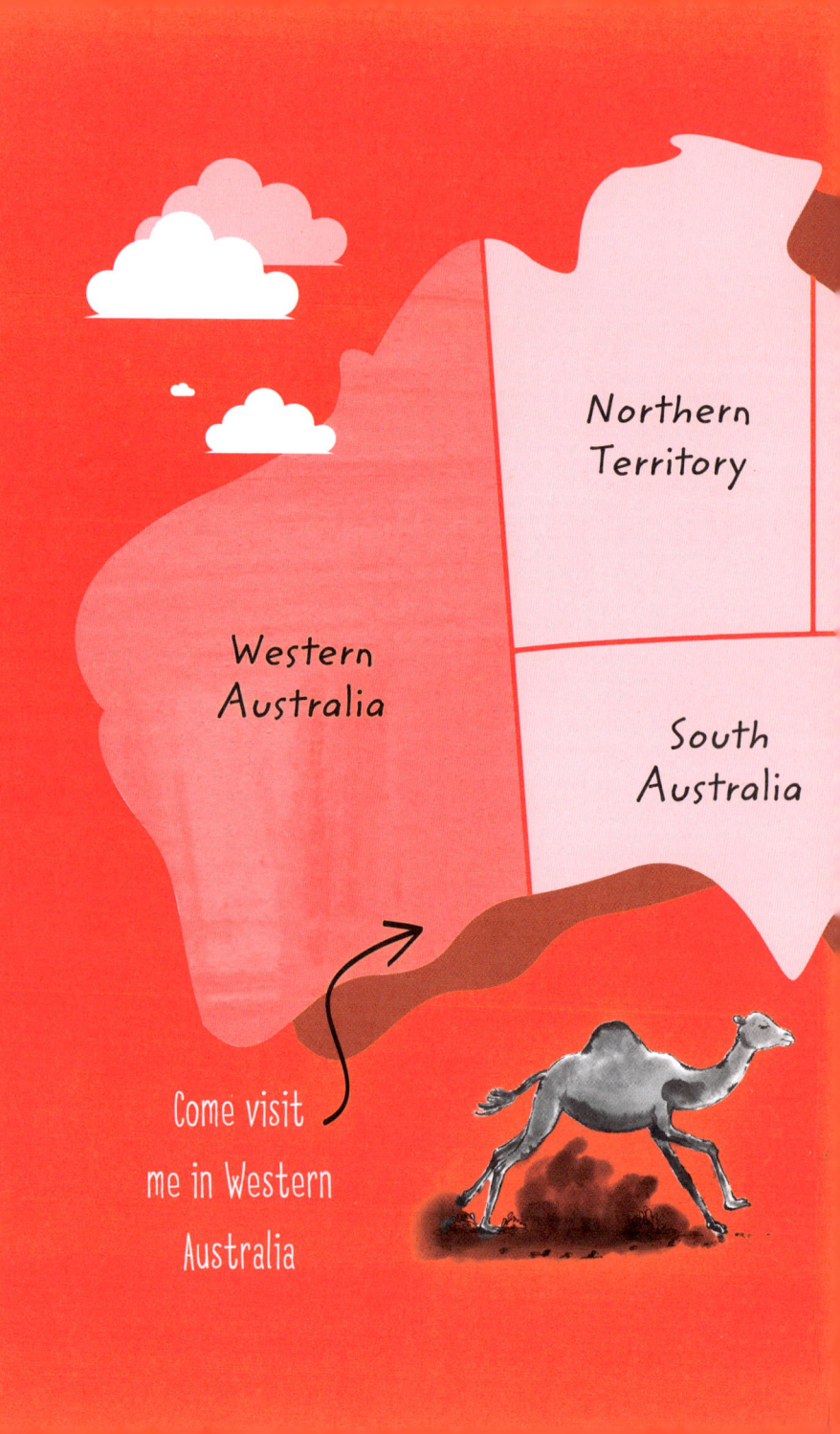

Western Australia

South Australia

Come visit me in Western Australia

Australia

Queensland

New South Wales

ACT

Victoria

Tasmania

Hi! I'm Eve

POSTCARD

Hi,

I'm Eve! If you ever drive from one side of Australia to the other you'll probably find yourself at Nowhere. It's a magical place. You can have a cup of tea with 200 kangaroos. At night you can watch the universe go by. There are even camels and astronauts! Why don't you stop and say hello...

Eve

FROM:

Eve

Nowhere Roadhouse

Nullarbor Plain

Western Australia

Australia

Chapter 1

Popping Next Door

Dad said Nowhere Roadhouse was just a stop for people buying petrol and pies on the loneliest road in Western Australia. But it was Eve's home. And she thought it was magic.

She'd loved sharing the magic of Nowhere with Nan last year. She still couldn't believe Nan had come! The bus trip from Perth had taken fourteen hours!

But they'd had a great time feeding Bluey the blue-tongue lizard. Then they'd laughed at Brian the mudlark fighting with his own reflection in the petrol pumps.

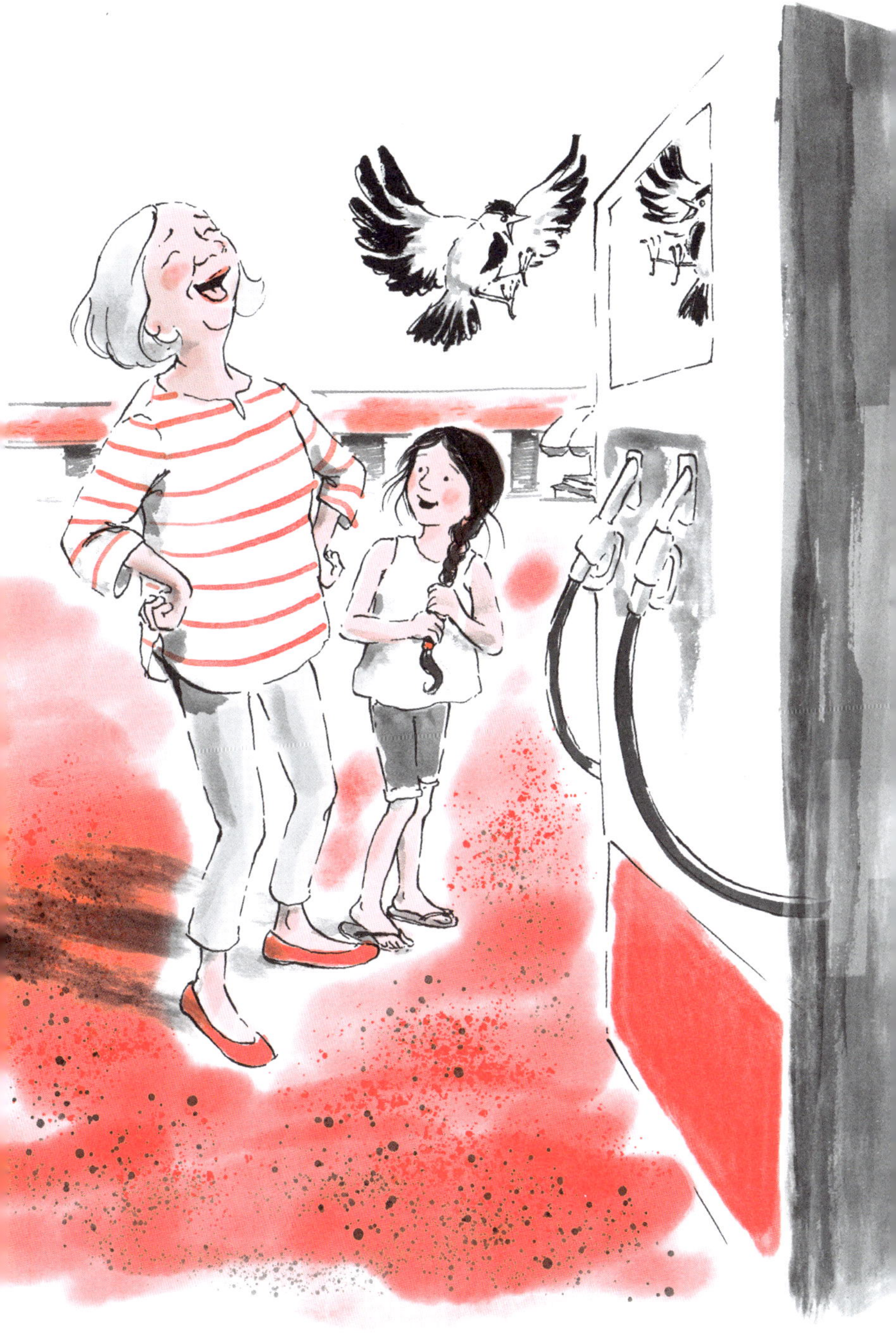

Nan said her favourite
part was having a cup of tea
with the kangaroos while
they enjoyed their sips of
breakfast dew . . .

Cousin Will was coming with Nan this year though. There were *dolphins* in the river next to his house.

Eve was afraid roos and blue-tongues and mudlarks couldn't possibly be as exciting as dolphins.

'What are we going to do with Will when he gets here?' she asked Dad.

'We'll pop next door, I think,' Dad said and smiled.

Eve grinned. It was perfect. There was nothing more magical than going to see *their* neighbour.

Chapter 2

Bush Magic

Nan and Will arrived on the late bus. There was hardly time for a hug before bed. Eve was disappointed, but the next morning Nan came and woke her up. She kissed Eve's nose.

'Let's go and show Will the car graveyard!' Nan said excitedly.

Eve wasn't sure. She thought Will would want to do something more exciting.

How much magic could there be in a pile of rusty, broken-down wrecks?

Will found plenty though! For him the wrecks were all racing cars!

Next they had breakfast –
a feast of Nan's heavenly
hash browns with Cook's
bonzer bacon burgers.

'Right!' Dad said. 'Who's up
for a drive to Doug's place?'

They piled into the ute.

Nan waved them off. She was staying behind to look after the roadhouse.

'Don't worry about me!' she said. 'Cook's going to teach me how to make his wicked wedges!'

They set off, but Will quickly got bored. There was nothing to look at. Hardly even a tree.

Neighbours weren't really 'next door' out here either. Doug's gate was forty minutes away. Then there was the long driveway.

Eve was getting a bit bored herself when suddenly, out of nowhere, magic happened!

A camel went galumphing past, flattening the saltbush and kicking up a cloud of thick, red dust.

'Wow!' Will said, his eyes popping.

Eve smiled. Thank goodness. Will might have dolphins where he lived, but it looked like camels were pretty exciting too.

Chapter 3

Chores are Fun!

After they saw the camel, Will kept watch out the window for more bush magic. He was the one who spotted Doug's gate. Just in time too! If they'd blinked they would have missed it.

They opened their mouths and went 'ah, a, a, a, a, a, a,' all the way down the long drive. The bumps in the dirt made their voices vibrate and their bones feel like they were rattling in their bodies.

When they got to the homestead, Dad introduced Will to Doug.

'So what's the plan?' Dad asked.

'A few chores to start with I think,' Doug replied.

Will looked a bit worried, but Eve wasn't. She'd helped Doug with the chores before. It was great!

Kangaroos flew ahead of them as they drove across the paddocks.

Whenever they drove over a clump of spinifex or saltbush, *boing!* Up they'd go. Then, *thud!* Down they'd come.

Will was really having fun now.

Doug took them to see some newborn lambs. He had to make sure mother and baby were both doing fine.

Then they stopped to check that there was water in the troughs.

After that they helped a sheep who was caught in the fencing wire.

'Must have seen a greener blade of grass on the other side!' Doug joked.

Eve shaded her eyes and looked around. There weren't many blades of grass at all that she could see. Just kilometre after kilometre of flat red dirt and, above it, the wide blue outback sky.

Chapter 4

Staying in Touch

Next they took Will to see the old telegraph station.

'Messages used to be sent along a single wire strung across hundreds of telegraph poles in those days,' Doug explained.

'It was all there was connecting one side of the country to the other.'

'And the folk that lived here had to make sure the wire never got broken,' Dad added.

Will had a mobile phone so he could call his mum, and Eve could see him trying to imagine the whole of Australia relying on one thin wire.

They played hide-and-seek in the spooky, abandoned rooms. Dry, cracked floorboards creaked and groaned. Eve thought she saw a ghost flitting down the hall...

'Boo!' went Will.

She was still laughing when Dad called them for lunch.

Cook had packed cold meat and pickle sandwiches. They sat out on the verandah.

'What's that?' Will asked, pointing.

Way off on the horizon a thin plume of smoke rose into the sky.

'That'll be Wally Scuds,' said Doug. 'Last dogger on the Nullarbor . . .'

Chapter 5

Tea and Treats

Everyone knew about Wally. He'd spent his whole life in the bush, sleeping in a swag under the stars. His job was to stop wild dogs from killing the sheep. He travelled thousands of kilometres doing it.

He'd once been married,
but now he lived alone. Wally
was never sad though. He
had a little dog for company
and he'd once told Eve he'd
lived a lucky life.

Eve was thrilled! She had hoped that Will would get to meet Wally.

When they pulled up at the camp fire, Eve jumped out of the ute.

She had a special treat for Wally. Cook had packed it, just in case.

'Mmmmm,' Wally said, peeling back the wrapper. 'A Cherry Ripe sure beats a lump of manky mutton!'

Wally took a bite then turned to Will. 'Fancy a cup of billy tea, young fella?'

Wally sent Eve and Will to pick five perfect gum leaves for the tea.

'Chuck them in!' he said. 'Give it that bit of dinkum Aussie flavour.'

He added two handfuls of black tea-leaves. Then he put on a glove, reached for the handle, and lifted the billy off the camp fire.

'Secret to brewing the perfect cuppa,' he said, swinging his arm right around with the billy. 'Spin her round like a propeller. Make it fast 'n do it like you mean it.'

Will's eyes popped right out of his head this time.

'Wow!' he said. 'You didn't spill a drop! Even when it was upside-down!'

Eve couldn't stop grinning.

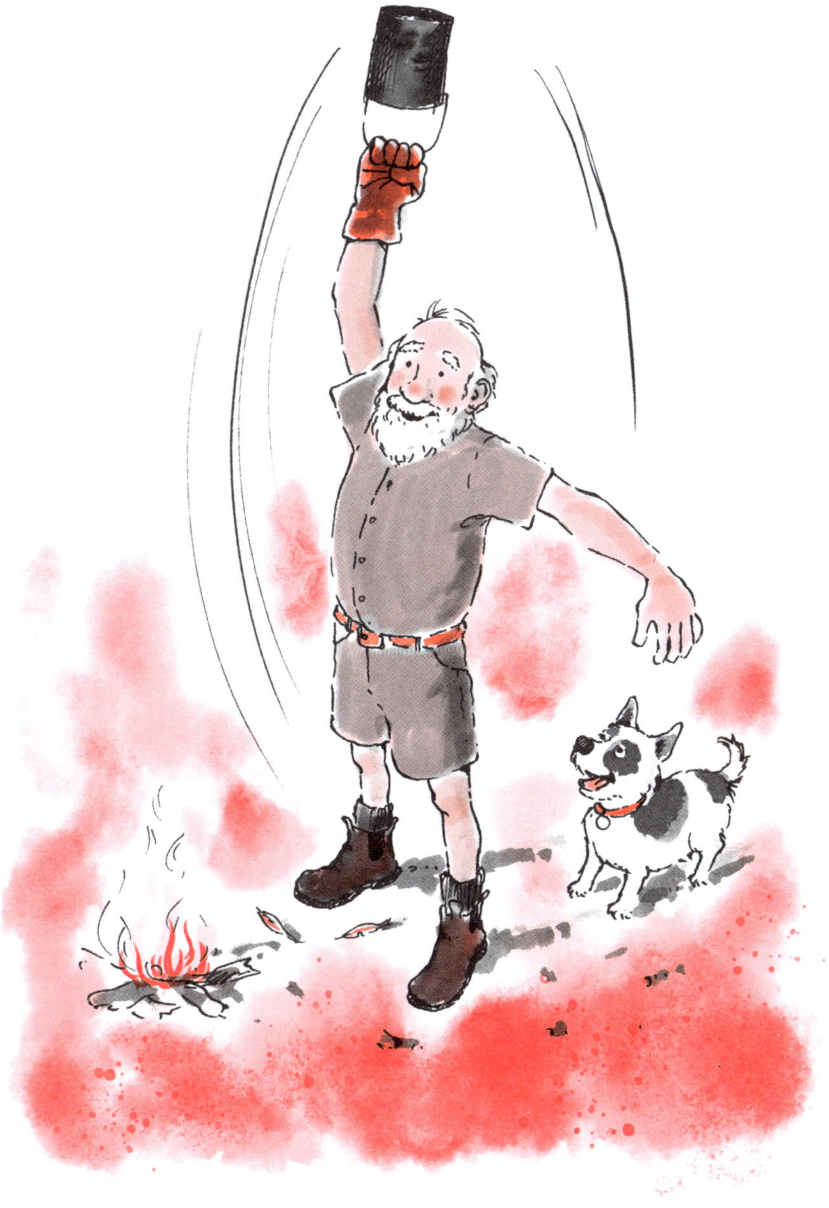

Dad was grinning too.

'And that's today's science lesson,' Doug said, and laughed.

Chapter 6

Golden Hour

It was getting late by the time they said goodbye to Wally and his dog. But they still had one more special place to see. Afghan Rocks. The most beautiful waterhole in the Nullarbor.

When they arrived everything was bathed in a glorious yellowy orange light.

Even the air seemed to glow.

'Golden hour,' sighed Dad.

Will and Eve climbed all over the sun-warmed rocks. They found flat lizards that weren't afraid of them at all. There were scattered pools of sparkling, icy water.

They cupped their hands and splashed their faces.

Finally, while the sun set in a breathtaking gold-bullion blaze, Doug told them about the people the waterhole was named after.

'There was no highway back then,' he said. 'No telegraph station either. Just camel trains led by strong, brave Afghan men who'd already come from half a world away.'

Eve looked at Will. She hoped he'd had as much fun as she'd had today. She hoped Will would want to come again with Nan.

But most of all, she hoped he saw the real magic of Nowhere.

Chapter 7

Next to Nowhere

Back at Doug's homestead they had dinner out on the porch – floury damper and lamb stew with fizzy, homemade ginger beer.

'I'm so hungry I could eat an old boot,' said Dad.

Eve smiled thinking about what Nan and Cook might be having back at the roadhouse. Nan's splendid spaghetti or Cook's beaut butter chook?!

When everyone was finished, Dad cleared away the dishes. Eve washed and Will dried then Doug went and got his old guitar. Dad fetched his harmonica from the glove box.

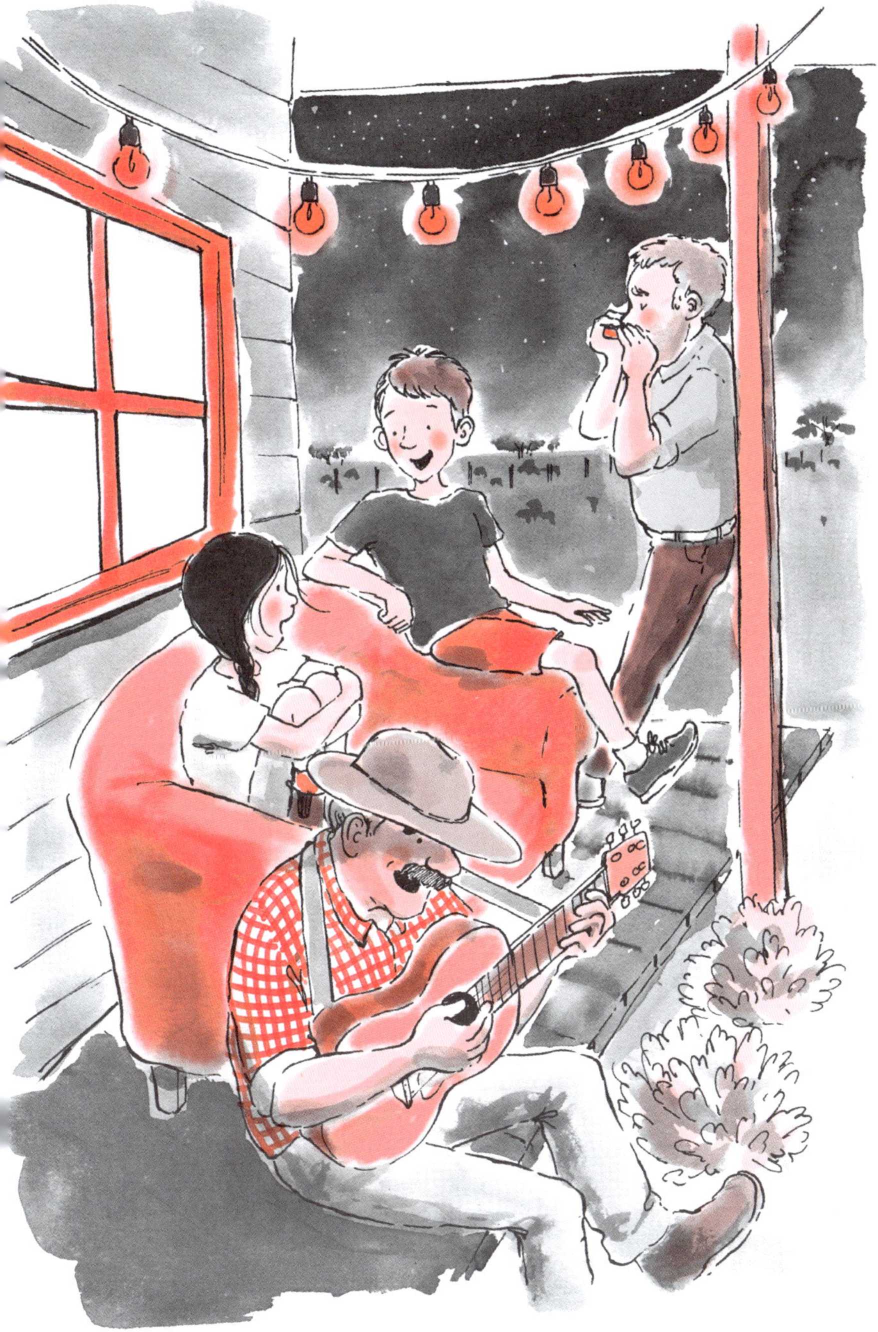

The night was so still, Eve thought Wally and his little dog could probably hear the music.

At last Doug ran out of songs. A trillion stars twinkled overhead.

He showed Will the Southern Cross and explained how you could use the pointers to find your way home if you ever got lost.

A shooting star zapped across the sky.

Suddenly, Eve spotted the International Space Station!

'Look!' she cried. 'Astronauts!'

'Well, blow me down,' said Dad. 'The Queen's going to turn up next.'

They laughed and then while Doug and Dad discussed tomorrow's weather, Eve curled up on the porch couch. It was all so nice, so full of love and warmth and wonder.

She was starting to nod off when she heard Will quietly ask her something that made a joyful little firework pop and sparkle in her heart.

'Is there anywhere else in the world you'd rather live?' Will asked with a sigh.

Eve gave her cousin a happy, sleepy smile.

'Next to Nowhere, Will,' she whispered.

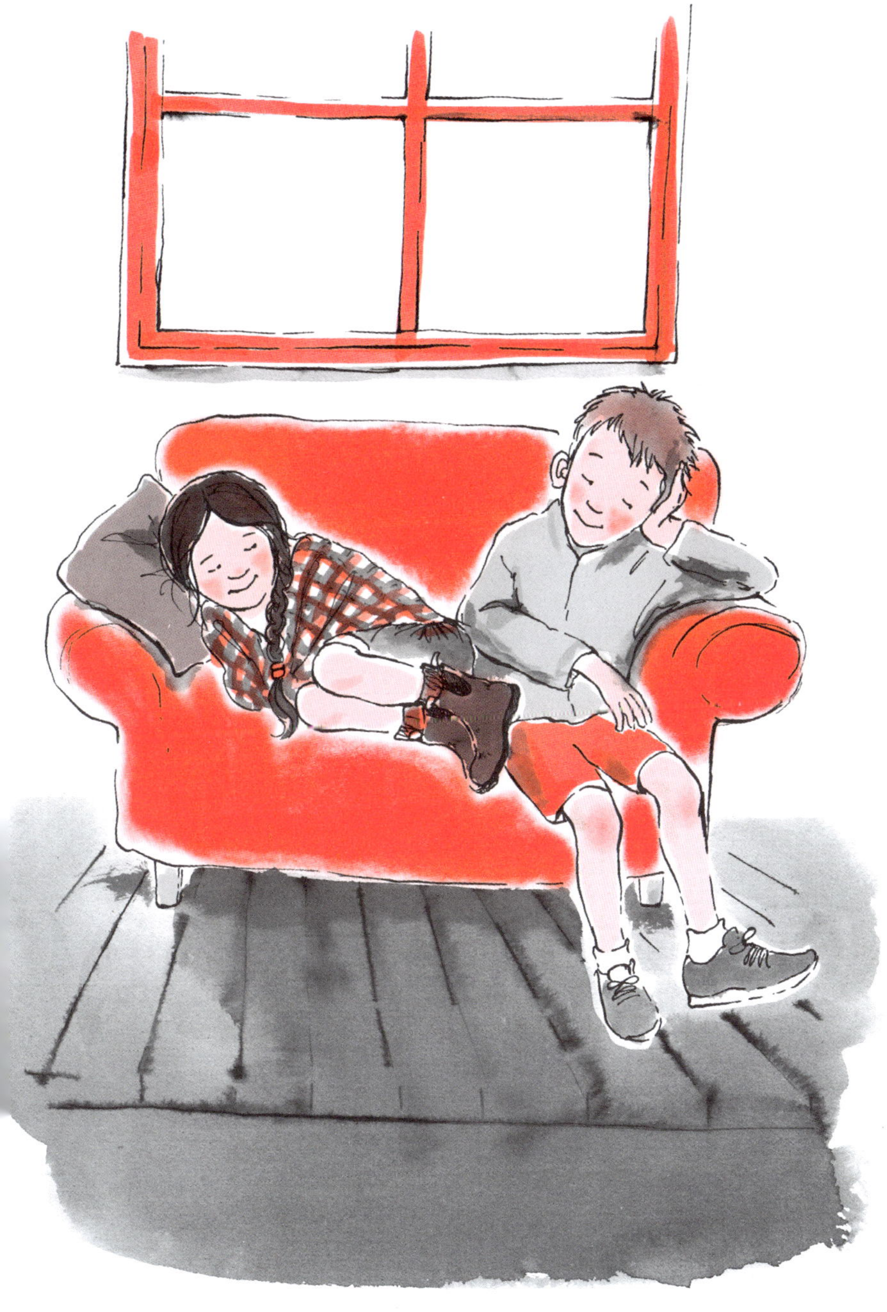

Fun Facts
About the Outback

Camels
Before real trains crossed the Nullarbor there were only camel trains! Today 100,000 wild camels roam the plains.

90 mile straight
Eve lives at one end of the longest straight road in Australia. It is 146.6 kilometres long!

Why doesn't Wally spill the tea?

The force of the tea pushing on the bottom of the billy is stronger than the force of gravity. But only if it's swung fast enough!

About the AUTHOR

I actually lived at Nowhere so I guess you could say, Eve is me! I knew Doug too. He was the one who told me to bring Wally a Cherry Ripe. Now I live where Will does and there are dolphins in the river next to my house. I think dolphins might be cooler than camels, but only because they live in water!

About the ILLUSTRATOR

I love where I live in Fremantle, Western Australia. I am near the Swan River, where I sometimes see dolphins — just like Will! But I also love the WA outback where there is so much space. The rocks, fences and sheep make little patterns in the vast, dry landscape.

Meet More Aussie Kids

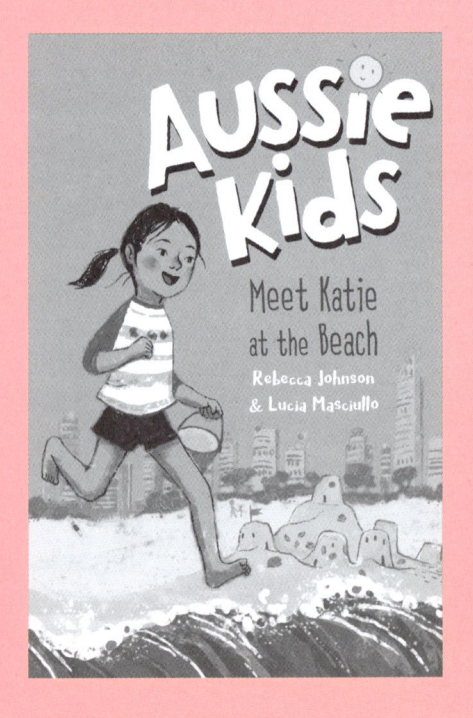

Meet Katie at the Beach

I have a wobbly tooth that won't come out! But it's not going to spoil my trip to the beach. We're going to eat mangoes and play beach cricket!

Meet Taj at the Lighthouse

This is my favourite T-shirt. I brought it to Australia from my old home. My family came here after a long journey. It was hard at first, but now I love my new home!

Meet Zoe and Zac at the Zoo

We're so lucky we live at the zoo! As a birthday treat, we're helping out with the animals. We can't wait!

Tick the Aussie Kids books you have read:

○ **Meet Eve in the Outback**
Raewyn Caisley & Karen Blair

○ **Meet Taj at the Lighthouse**
Maxine Beneba Clarke & Nicki Greenberg

○ **Meet Zoe and Zac at the Zoo**
Belinda Murrell & David Hardy

○ **Meet Katie at the Beach**
Rebecca Johnson & Lucia Masciullo

○ **Meet Sam at the Mangrove Creek**
Paul Seden & Brenton McKenna

○ **Meet Mia by the Jetty**
Janeen Brian & Danny Snell

○ **Meet Dooley on the Farm**
Sally Odgers & Christina Booth

○ **Meet Matilda at the Festival**
Jacqueline de Rose-Ahern & Tania McCartney